A VALENTINE FOR FRANKENSTEIN

An icky-eyeball cupcake for Alix,
my monstrously marvelous editor
—L.K.

A valentine for my three little monsters
—T.B.

Carolrhoda Books
A division of Lerner Publishing Group, Inc.
241 First Avenue North
Minneapolis, MN 55401 USA

For reading levels and more information, look up this title at www.lernerbooks.com.

Designed by Kimberly Morales.
Main body text set in Coventry ITC Std 18/18.
Typeface provided by International Typeface Corporation.
The digital illustrations in this book were created with Photoshop.

Library of Congress Cataloging-in-Publication Data

Names: Kimmelman, Leslie, author. | Banks, Timothy, illustrator.
Title: A valentine for Frankenstein / Leslie Kimmelman ; illustrated by Timothy Banks.
Description: Minneapolis : Carolrhoda Books, [2018] | Summary: Frankenstein stands out
    at the Valentine's Day Bash for being less monstrous than the other guests, but to one
    smelly, rude creature that makes him the perfect valentine.
Identifiers: LCCN 2017040105 (print) | LCCN 2017053239 (ebook) | ISBN 9781541523715
    (eb pdf) | ISBN 9781512431292 (lb : alk. paper)
Subjects: | CYAC: Monsters—Fiction. | Parties—Fiction. | Individuality—Fiction. |
    Valentine's Day—Fiction.
Classification: LCC PZ7.K56493 [ebook] | LCC PZ7.K56493 Val 2018 (print) | DDC [E]—dc23

LC record available at https://lccn.loc.gov/2017040105

Manufactured in the United States of America
1-41705-23519-2/14/2018

A VALENTINE FOR FRANKENSTEIN

LESLIE
KIMMELMAN

illustrated by
TIMOTHY
BANKS

Carolrhoda Books • Minneapolis

All over town, monsters were getting ready for the Valentine's Day Bash:

taking slime baths . . .

teasing and tangling their tails . . .

and sharpening their claws and fangs.

In his castle, Frankenstein was getting ready too.

He looked in the mirror.

His skin was a ghastly shade of green.

His head was an almost perfect square.

His flower was droopy and near dead.

Still, the other monsters all made fun of him.

"Just two eyes!" said Smellabella.

"No tail," said Werewolf. "He looks almost . . . human!"

"And he's **nice**," sneered Spike. "Blech!"

"I don't believe he's a monster at all!" said Brains.

But Frankenstein was comfortable in his own green skin.
So he stitched on his crookedest smile,

dressed in his worst tuxedo,
and set off for the party.

The cupcake-decorating contest was first.

Three-Eyed Vy made a cupcake called
This Icky Eyeball Is Watching You.

Wartina's creation had fungus filling and toenail frosting.

Frankenstein made the grossest
cupcake he could think of.

He held it up to the judges and smiled.

"You call **that** a monster cupcake?" Smellabella jeered.

"No bugs?"

"No slime?"

"And glitter on top?"

Three-Eyed Vy threw a cupcake at his face.

"Bull's-eye!" said Frankenstein.
"Good aim, Vy."

Next came the banana-slug pie-eating contest.

Frankenstein was super speedy.

He thought he would win—until he wiped his mouth with a napkin and was immediately disqualified.

"That's not how monsters eat, buster," Spike snickered.

He put a pie on the floor, stomped on it, and then snarfed the pieces from between his hairy toes.

"That's how monsters eat."

"Wow!" said Frankenstein admiringly. "You're very talented."

The last contest was for burping.

Frankenstein's was the loudest, longest, smelliest burp he'd ever made.

"You call that a burp?" said Stinker. "That was a cough! A hiccup! It was almost a giggle!"

Just then, a monster burped so loudly the ground shook.

"Way to go, Belcher!" yelled Smellabella. "That was epic!"

Frankenstein had never seen Belcher before.

She was taller than he was, with piles of tangled black hair and a beautiful smile.

"Awesome," said Frankenstein, smitten.

But before Frankenstein could congratulate Belcher on her terrifically disgusting, award-winning burp, the band began to play.

The monsters were wild about dancing.

Mummies unwrapped.

Fangs flew.

A skeleton named Bones fell to pieces.

Luckily, Frankenstein was there to lend a hand.

Belcher boogied like a pro.

Frankenstein tried to copy her moves.
But during the zombie rhumba, he fell flat
on his face.

It was hard to rhumba with two left feet.

When he stood up, he noticed something sticking out of his pocket.
IT WAS A VALENTINE'S DAY CARD!

For me? thought Frankenstein.

It was his first valentine ever.

Which ghoul could have put
it there?

"Was it you, Rainbow?" he asked, holding up the card.

Rainbow answered by spitting at him in five colors.

"Impressive," said Frankenstein, cleaning his face with his handkerchief and sighing softly.

"As if," said Headless Harriet, before he could ask.

Then she removed her head and threw some purple glop at him.

The soft glop didn't hurt, though his feelings did.
Still, "Cool color!" Frankenstein managed to reply.

Frankenstein searched the card for clues.

The card was zigzag shaped.

The writing was red.

It had the whiff of something stinky and wonderful.

Just then Belcher bopped by.

She had a red marker in her pocket.

She had a zigzag stripe in her hair.

She had a wonderful stinky smell wafting off her.

She had to be his secret valentine!

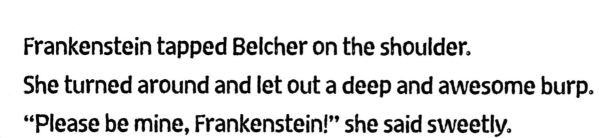

Frankenstein tapped Belcher on the shoulder.

She turned around and let out a deep and awesome burp.

"Please be mine, Frankenstein!" she said sweetly.

Frankenstein grinned so widely some stitches popped.

He gave Belcher a worm wristband.

She gave Frankenstein a piece of snot-flavored bubble gum.

The other monsters noticed . . . and wondered.

What did Belcher see in him?

"I've never met a **friendly** monster before," gushed Belcher. "He's **my** kind of monster!"

"He did notice my perfect aim," said Three-Eyed Vy slowly.

"And my monster manners," observed Spike.

"His extra body parts come in hand-y," mumbled Bones.

"I guess it's okay to be nice—sometimes," Headless Harriet added, remembering that Frankenstein had liked her purple glop.

"If that's the kind of monster you are."

The music started up again.

The monsters joined together in a ginormous kicking, spitting, burping, gnashing, glitter-tastic conga line.

Every kind of monster was welcome.

After all,
a monster . . .
is a monster . . .
is a monster.